DOROTHY HINSHAW PATENT

A FAMILY GOES HUNTING

Photographs by
WILLIAM MUÑOZ

CLARION BOOKS • NEW YORK

To the memory of Ann Troy,
who encouraged us on this project

Clarion Books
a Houghton Mifflin Company imprint
215 Park Avenue South, New York, NY 10003
Text copyright © 1991 by Dorothy Hinshaw Patent
Photographs copyright © 1991 by William Muñoz

Library of Congress Cataloging-in-Publication Data
Patent, Dorothy Hinshaw.
 A family goes hunting / by Dorothy Hinshaw Patent ; photographs by William Muñoz.
  p. cm.
 Summary: Relates, in text and photographs, the experiences of twelve-year-old Leif
as he goes on his first hunting trip with his family in Montana.
 ISBN 0–395–52004–5
 1. Hunting – Montana – Juvenile literature. 2. Hunting – Montana – Pictorial works –
Juvenile literature. [1. Hunting.] I. Muñoz, William, ill. II. Title.
SK99.P38 1991
799.29786 – dc20   90–28301
                                         CIP   AC

ISBN 0-395-52004-5 PA ISBN 0-395-66507-8

HOR 10 9 8 7 6 5 4 3

CONTENTS

INTRODUCTION

When I moved to Montana in 1972, I was surprised to discover how many people I met were hunters. I wondered about them – how could they shoot wild animals? I couldn't understand why they would want to do such a thing. But the fact that so many of the fine people I came to know looked forward with great enthusiasm to the hunting season seemed to suggest that I should get to know more about the sport. One of my first new friends, Gene Hansen, grew up with hunting. His early memories are of following his father through the woods tracking deer. Through long conversations with Gene and others, I have come to understand something of what hunting means to those who pursue it.

Hunting provides a way of feeling part of nature. Hunters enjoy just being outdoors, smelling the fresh scent of the woods, being alert to signs that wild animals are around, and getting a good workout walking for miles. But the experience of hunting an animal provides an even deeper sense of connection with the natural world.

The hunters I know have very strong feelings about what is

right and what is wrong when it comes to hunting. They all make certain that what they kill is eaten and not wasted. Many families count on the game they gather during the hunting season to provide them with meat throughout the year. Some of these people haven't tasted beef or chicken for years!

I also understand how hunting can play an important role in maintaining a balanced ecology. The human hunter takes the part of a wild predator, such as a wolf or mountain lion. Like the lion, the hunter must stalk the elusive prey, using his or her knowledge of the wild and the habits of the prey to find it. Prey animals are far from helpless. Evolution over countless generations has sharpened their senses and given them ways to hide themselves and to escape their predators. They also learn fast about the habits and methods of human foes. All these factors make hunting a genuine challenge.

Since humans don't have a good sense of smell for tracking, they use dogs to help them hunt some prey, such as birds. (In many states, it is illegal to use dogs in hunting big game like deer.) A wolf or mountain lion has built-in weapons – long, pointed canine teeth and, in the case of the lion, strong, sharp claws. People lack such weapons, so they use bows and arrows or guns to kill. But the human hunter's most important weapon is intelligence. Human hunters feel that they have met the challenge of the wild when they discover ways to outsmart their prey. Hunting intelligence does not guarantee success, however. Many times hunters come home empty-handed, but with a great sense of respect for the animals that have eluded them.

Of course, hunting, like any other activity, attracts irresponsible people as well as those who are responsible. Some hunters aren't careful with their guns and end up shooting themselves or other people as a result. Others don't respect the game and try to get away with exceeding the bag limits, or use irresponsible or illegal hunting methods, such as spotlighting animals at night. These people give hunting a bad name.

I have not discussed the controversial aspects of hunting here – that would be a book in itself, a much longer and more complicated book than this one. Problems associated with trophy-hunting contests, killing Yellowstone bison when they leave the park, hunting in populated areas, poaching, and so forth are all important issues that need to be dealt with, but they are not the focus of this book. Here I have focused on hunting as a healthy family activity.

I believe strongly that most hunters are like my friends, Gene Hansen and the Cox family. For them, hunting is a sport that brings them together in shared outdoor activities, provides them with opportunities to teach children responsibility and cooperation, and results in a healthy life-style. Hunting affords them a diet of meat low in fat and lacking contaminants that are in meat from animals raised in crowded domesticated conditions. One purpose in writing this book was to provide information about hunting. But much more important, I wanted nonhunters to have the opportunity to know the positive side of hunting.

I use the Cox family's experiences hunting pheasant and deer to give a picture of what hunting is like. But there is much more to meat hunting than deer and pheasant. Elk, moose, antelope, mountain goat, bighorn sheep, sometimes bear, and a variety of birds are also hunted for their meat.

Every state has its own set of laws and rules governing hunting. In addition to regulating when and where hunting is allowed, state laws affect how much licenses cost, what weapons can be used (for example, some states allow deer hunting with shotguns while others don't), how many animals can be taken, what sex of animals can be hunted, and other details. The focus of most of these rules is on using hunting to keep the populations of hunted birds and mammals healthy.

In addition, many of the rules concern safety. For example, states like Montana require that all big-game hunters and those accompanying them must wear 400 square inches of hunter orange, which is very bright and fluorescent. Also, hunters are not allowed to shoot from cars or outside established shooting hours, as safety precautions.

In many states, including Montana, hunters are forbidden to waste any edible part of a game animal. The meat must be taken with the intention of eating it.

Much of the money collected from licensing is used to help in wildlife management. Some licensing money goes for buying land that many kinds of animals, not just game species, need — such as wetlands in which ducks and other waterfowl breed. The National Wildlife Refuge system, for example, which provides critical habitat for countless animals, began as an effort to preserve land for hunted waterfowl and is financed in large part by money collected from hunters. Without the money contributed by hunters, both publicly and privately, toward wildlife preservation, millions of acres now set aside would have been drained for agricultural use, subdivided, or turned into malls and parking lots.

1

THE
COX FAMILY

*T*he Cox family of Montana – father Roger, mother Carla, and children Leif and Heidi – love the outdoors and outdoor activities: skiing, canoeing, mountain biking, climbing. Most of all, the Coxes enjoy hunting together, along with their dogs – Greta, an English pointer, and Max, a Labrador retriever.

Roger Cox has hunted since he was a boy. "I learned to hunt from my dad, and he learned from his father," Roger says. "Hunting has always been an important part of life in my family. I like getting outdoors with my family, seeing wild country, and learning together. I especially enjoy the challenge – the need to keep all my senses alert, to be smart enough to get an opportunity for a shot. Whether or not I actually shoot and kill the animal is not as important as getting that chance. Making a killing shot – that's more like target practice. It's successfully stalking the animal that provides the challenge."

"When I met Roger," Carla adds, "he was in graduate school studying economics. He had his classes arranged so he could get away during hunting season. When he asked me to marry him,

Leif and Heidi Cox love sports like mountain biking.

The Coxes' English pointer, Greta (left), moves like a graceful dancer. Their Labrador retriever, Max (right), is a happy, energetic dog.

Roger Cox is an economist.   *Carla is a dietitian.*

he said there was one thing I'd have to do first – swim one hundred yards with a bird in my mouth! I didn't do that, but we still got married."

Roger taught Carla to hunt, and Leif and Heidi have been going along on hunting trips ever since they were babies. They have learned right from the start how to hunt safely and with respect for the animals.

Leif is now twelve, old enough to hunt legally, but he couldn't just go out and do it because he had reached legal age. First he had to pass a course in hunter safety sponsored by the state Department of Fish and Game. The classes are given after school or

 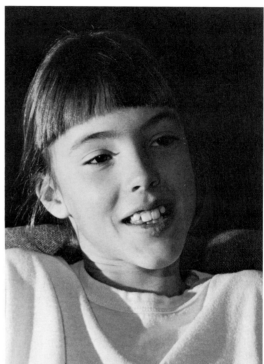

Leif (left) *is glad he's old enough to hunt. Heidi* (right) *enjoys hunting with her family, even though she isn't old enough to use a gun.*

in the evenings. Young hunters are taught how to handle guns safely and how to survive in the wild if they get lost. After taking the class, the students must pass an examination to make sure they understand what they need to know to be responsible, safe hunters.

Heidi is only eight, so she has a wooden gun. But she must carry that gun as if it were real. By the time she is old enough to shoot, safe hunting practices will be completely natural to Heidi. "I like hunting," says Heidi. "It's fun because it's adventuring."

The Coxes don't hunt just because it's fun. "My father died of a heart attack when he was only sixty-four years old, so I'm concerned about my health and the health of my family," Carla explains. "I'm a dietitian and know what foods are good for you. Animal fat can be bad for the heart, and wild game has very little fat. It also hasn't been exposed to the hormones and antibiotics given to domesticated cattle and chickens. Though it isn't

Children who want to hunt must take hunter safety classes where they learn about survival in the woods, among other things.

proven, there's evidence that suggests those chemicals may be harmful to eat."

Carla's concern for healthy eating includes everything her family eats. The Coxes have a garden every year.

"In our own garden, we can raise vegetables organically. We can eat them when they are very fresh. We also can and freeze vegetables for winter eating. See the tall fence around the garden? That's to keep out the deer. Before we put up the fence, gardening around here was very chancy. Sometimes the deer ate just about everything."

"Before the white man came along," adds Roger, "wild predators like wolves controlled the populations of game animals like deer and elk. Now most of the predators are gone. Without hunting, there would be too many deer. In each state, officials determine how many animals can be killed by hunters in each area. That way, the populations of game animals are kept under control."

$\sim$2

GUNS AND BULLETS

*H*unting requires a lot of preparation. Hunters can't just go out on the first day of the season and shoot a deer or elk. There is work to be done first. Hunters must take care of their guns properly when not using them, and get them ready before the beginning of each season.

"We always keep our guns in this locked, out-of-the-way closet, unloaded and zipped up in their cases," says Roger. "The ammunition is stored separately. We see no reason for display-

Roger explains about guns and safety.

Roger aims his double-barreled shotgun.

ing the guns in a locked cabinet the way many people do. Our guns are not for show, they are for hunting, and our children understand that.

"We use different kinds of guns for hunting. Shotguns are for shooting game birds like pheasant and ducks. A shotgun shell releases a cluster of small metal pellets, which makes it easier to hit birds in flight. In states with lots of people, shotguns may also be used for hunting deer, because their range is short. That way, there is less chance that someone will be hit accidentally by a shot that misses. There are special solid lead slugs and shells with only a few large pellets that are used for deer hunting.

"Rifles are for shooting big game like deer and elk. Each time I shoot my rifle, a single metal bullet heads toward the target. Bullets are very effective at killing big game quickly. And rifles have a much longer range than shotguns.

The family cross a fence with their rifles on a deer hunt. Notice that Carla holds Roger's rifle as he goes under the fence.

"Both rifle cartridges and shotgun shells can be reloaded and used again. We shoot our rifles so seldom that it isn't worth re-loading our cartridges. But we do reload our shotgun shells, since it's so much less expensive that way."

Roger points to a complicated-looking gadget on the table. "This is the reloader. To reload the shell, the first thing is to punch out the old primer at the base of the shell and put a new one in. Then you've got an empty shell, with just the primer.

"The next step is to put the powder in, a specific amount of powder, depending on the kind of shell. Then on top of it you put in this plastic piece called a wad. The wad holds the shot pellets. Finally you close the shell by crimping the end to hold everything in."

While Roger talks, Leif crimps the shells for this season's hunt. "When the gun fires, the firing pin strikes the primer, igniting it, like lighting a match. That sends a spark into the powder, which ignites and burns. That creates pressure, forcing the wad and shot to fly out toward the target. When the shot leaves the shell, it's traveling at about twelve hundred feet per second. The wind catches the wad and it drops off. The farther the shot goes, the more the pellets separate and the bigger the pattern."

Roger takes out a box of rifle ammunition. "A rifle works in the same way. You call each piece of rifle ammunition a round. The round is similar to the shotgun shell, but it doesn't have a wad, and it has just one pointed metal bullet that leaves the shell and heads toward the target. Otherwise, it's the same thing.

"Reloading is really very complicated. There are hundreds of ways of reloading and dozens of kinds of bullets, each designed for a particular use."

It's important for hunters to take good care of their equip-

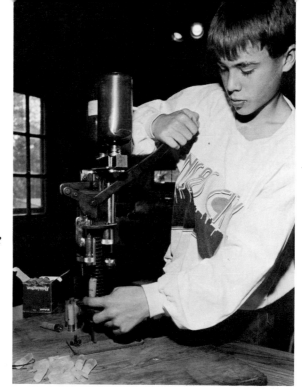

Leif positions a shotgun shell so the reloader can close the end. The plastic objects in the lower left are wads.

When Leif pushes down on the handle, the reloader firmly crimps down the top of the shell.

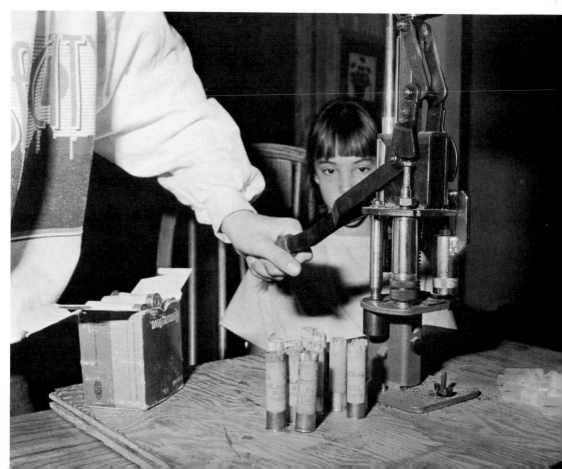

Shotgun shells and rifle rounds look different, but they work in the same way. Notice the primer in the center of the end of each kind of ammunition.

Leif breaks open his shotgun for cleaning.

At the end of the season, Leif cleans his gun again; here he is cleaning the inside of the barrel. Notice that even when the gun is completely broken apart, he aims the barrel away from himself.

ment. Roger explains, "Guns need to be cleaned and oiled several times during the season. They get one good cleaning at the beginning of the season and another at the end. If they get dusty or dirty on a trip, they must be cleaned again. Cleaning keeps the action working smoothly – a dirty or rusty gun can malfunction. A good hunter is proud of his equipment and wants to take good care of it, just like a nice bike or baseball glove.

"When we clean our guns, we clean them inside and out. We make sure that there aren't any bits of dirt inside the barrels that can interfere with our shooting. We oil the outside metal parts to protect them from rusting. Once our guns are carefully cleaned, they're ready to be used."

3

GETTING
INTO PRACTICE

"We start getting ready weeks before the hunting season begins each fall," Roger says. "We practice our shooting, and the dogs need to be reminded what to do."

"Especially Max," Carla adds. "He's just a young dog and is still learning. It's hard for him not to join in when he might get in Greta's way, and he still isn't sure how he feels about feathers in his mouth."

Roger hooks an old bird wing onto the end of a fishing line. He flips the wing this way and that, letting it rest on the ground long enough for Greta to see it and go into a point. Greta looks like a graceful dancer, leaping here and there, focusing on the wing, not letting it out of her sight. Meanwhile, Max is sitting on the sidelines, eager to join Greta but stopped with a stern "No" every time he tries to get up.

"Max needs to learn to honor Greta's point and not interfere," explains Roger. "He mustn't get in the way or bark in excitement. When a pointer points the bird, the hunter knows where the bird is and can get set to shoot. Then the bird is flushed and flies up where we can get a clean shot.

Roger uses an old bird wing on the end of a fishing line to work with Greta.

When the wing lands on the ground, Greta freezes into a point.

Carla tells Max that he must sit and leave Greta alone while she works.

When Max's turn comes, he brings back a dead bird enthusiastically.

"Greta and Max have separate jobs. They complement each other in the field. She ranges far and hunts by following the scent on the wind. She carries her head high and follows the wind currents. She uses her nose like a white-tailed deer does. She works upwind to the game, and when the scent reaches a certain intensity, she freezes and points until the bird moves or we flush it.

"Max hunts differently. He trails the scent left on the ground – he's a foot tracker. A bird can run right in front of him and he may not see it. He's got his head down in the weeds, smelling. You can see Greta running along a fence line with her head up and Max following right behind with his head down. While Greta's at her best in open country, where scents are carried by the wind, Max works well in heavy cover, where there's more to hold the scent."

Roger teaches Max how to drop the bird into his hand after retrieving it.

After working with the dogs, it is time for the hunters to refresh their skills. The dogs jump into their portable kennels in the back of the station wagon, the shooting gear is loaded, and the family drives to an open space in the woods by a sharp bend in a dirt country road. Neighbors in the area all use this clearing to practice shooting.

When everything is unloaded, the dogs are let out from their kennels and made to sit behind the shooters. Clay pigeons are to be the target today. These are disks made of clay that are launched one or two at a time from a special device. While Roger, Carla, and Leif practice shooting, Heidi mans the clay pigeon launcher.

"Ready? Go, Heidi!" calls out Carla. Heidi pulls on the rope and the pigeons sail through the air.

Since it is a cool day with a short drive, both Max and Greta are put into one large kennel for the ride to the shotgun practice spot.

Carla waits with her gun pointed up and the safety on while Heidi operates the clay pigeon launcher.

Bang! Bang! go the shotguns. Roger hits one pigeon, but Leif misses the other.

"You shot behind it, Leif. Let's try again. Ready? Go!"

Bang! Bang! again. Once more Roger hits and Leif misses.

"My wad hit it," says Leif.

The pigeons fly and Carla shoots.

"That means you shot in front of it that time," explains his father. "Now try again. Ready? Go!"

Heidi pulls the rope and out fly two more pigeons.

Bang! Bang!

"They both got hit, but I didn't shoot," says Roger.

"Neither did I," joins in Carla. Leif just stands there and smiles. "Leif shot 'em both – smart aleck!"

Roger explains an important difference between trap shooting

Leif shoots. Notice that he is leaning somewhat forward to help absorb the gun's recoil.

as a sport and as hunting practice. "Some trap shooters keep the safety off and the gun at their shoulder between shots. We're not doing that. We're getting used to our guns. We practice just like it will be when we're hunting." This makes hitting the pigeons much harder, for the shooters have to release the safety and swing the gun to their shoulder before aiming.

"A shooter has to lean forward a little because of the recoil," Roger continues. "Sometimes when I don't get my safety off or the gun misfires, I find myself staggering forward. Once you're used to shooting, you don't notice the recoil until it doesn't happen!"

As they practice, the Coxes have to keep reminding Max to sit still. "Get over here by Greta, Max — sit! That's it. Good girl, Greta, good girl," praises Roger, as Greta continues to sit quietly despite Max's nervousness.

"Max needs to get used to the sound of the guns," Roger explains. "He doesn't like it."

After a half hour's shooting, it is time to quit. "Okay, Greta and Max, you can go now," calls Carla, and the dogs take off running, circling around excitedly. Meanwhile, Heidi and Leif pick up the spent shells and put them in a box. "We can reuse these shells several times," says Roger. "And we always clean up after ourselves. Now let's let Max have some real fun. He's been pretty good about the shooting."

The family drives to the nearby freeway and soon exits at a rest stop. Everyone piles out of the car and skids down the slope to the river beach below. Leif carries along a rubber float, and Max wags his tail excitedly. "A Labrador retriever is a water dog, among the favorite breeds used for retrieving ducks and geese," Carla says. "Water is where Max loves most to be."

Leif and Heidi pick up the shells when shooting practice is over.

Roger and the children strip to their bathing suits. Leif tells Max to sit, then throws the float. Max's rear end barely touches the sand, and his front feet dance with excitement. He can hardly control himself. "Go fetch!" yells Leif, and Max springs into the water, swimming happily out to the float, taking it into his mouth, and paddling back. He drops the float into the sand

Leif throws the dummy for Max, who splashes into the water to retrieve it.

at Leif's feet. When the boy doesn't reach for it right away, Max starts to pick it up again, then drops it and begins pawing at it.

"He doesn't like sand in his mouth," Carla explains, laughing. "So he tries to roll it over to get the sand off, but all he does is get more sand on it." She reaches down for the float and tosses it into the water. Max cheerfully plunges in and goes after it.

An hour or so is enough on the beach for everyone except Max, but he has to go home with the rest of the family. It has been a busy day.

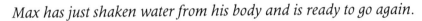

Max has just shaken water from his body and is ready to go again.

4

BIRD HUNTING

Mid-October to December is pheasant-hunting season in Montana. The Coxes hunt in the eastern part of the state, where game birds are plentiful. Roger's good friend John lives on a ranch there, and loves to join his friends to hunt pheasant. The Coxes always make sure they have permission when they hunt on someone's private property.

After a night in a nearby motel, the family gets up before dawn, eats a hearty breakfast, and heads out to John's place while it is still dark. John brings along his golden retriever, Buns, to help find birds. Pheasant hunters must be careful, since only male pheasant are legal to kill. Fortunately, the brightly colored male birds are very easy to recognize.

As the sky slowly brightens, the hunters get ready to head out. Hunting is legal from a half hour before sunrise until sunset.

"We'll spread out and work our way up this creek bed," explains Roger. "The pheasant live here under the cover of the bushes. The dogs will find them for us."

The group splits up and the hunt is on. Every few minutes whistles from the hunters directing the dogs ring through the still, cool morning air.

Leif waits for the hunt to begin, his shotgun safely broken open.

"Greta come, here Greta, come-come-come!" yells Roger.

"Over here, Buns," calls John.

The dogs run tirelessly, happily circling this way and that, noses to the ground. The dogs appear to swim through the grass, but it is rough going for the people, especially Heidi. The tall, heavy grass comes up to her shoulders. But she just keeps on walking.

"There's one of them right here," calls Leif. "It ran right by me."

Greta runs from the brush into a grassy area, searching for birds.

Heidi, John, and Buns hunt together.

"A pheasant?" asks Carla.

"Yeah, right here."

"Where's Greta?"

"She's with John."

By now the bird has run off through the bushes, and no one knows which way to look.

"Max, come on Max, come on you goof," calls Carla. Max appears in the brush, his head up, looking for his family. When he spies Carla, he comes running.

"Maxie, good boy!" praises Carla. Max is all wet. "Just like a retriever to head into the water if any's around!" Carla comments.

"Max doesn't know what he's doing!" adds Roger.

A moment later, Roger gets excited.

"Point? Leif! Look at Greta. We've got a point here – come on Leif, right here. She broke it, it's broken." The bird has run off through the brush, and Greta has broken her point and is stalking the bird instead of standing still in front of it.

"Come on," calls Roger. "We've got a bird ahead of us now."

Max responds to Carla's call by running to her.

Roger tells Leif to stop – there's a bird ahead.

Max works in front of Roger.

A male pheasant flies up after being flushed.

That bird manages to sneak away, but there are plenty of others. Every once in a while, the tip of a tail or an ear appears above the plants, showing where a dog is hunting through the thick underbrush. Greta catches the scent of a bird while Roger watches.

"Greta hold!" he cries.

Greta is frozen on point, one front leg raised and bent, her tail sticking straight out behind.

The hunters move up close to the dog, and the bird breaks into flight. The guns roar and the bird falls to the ground.

"Go fetch, Greta," calls Carla. Greta runs off and returns quickly, carrying the pheasant. She runs up to Roger, who takes the bird from her gentle mouth.

"Good girl, Greta, good girl!" praises Roger.

Everyone — except, of course, Heidi — has plenty of chances to bag pheasant this morning. Heidi and Leif are walking together when they come to a fence between two pastures.

"Hold my gun while I cross over, Heidi," asks Leif. When Leif has gone over the fence, Heidi carefully passes first her wooden

Roger takes a shot.

Greta gives Roger a pheasant she has retrieved.

gun and then his to him, and climbs over herself. It's especially important to be careful with guns while crossing fences. Careless hunters have been wounded or even killed by their guns while going over or under fences.

On the way back to the cars for lunch, Carla and Leif walk with Heidi along a dirt road, which is easier than going through the grass and brush.

Leif and Heidi help each other with their guns when crossing a fence.

Carla shows Heidi how to carry her gun safely.

"Leif," Carla asks, "do you remember when you were just four years old and carried your plastic gun when we went hunting? Heidi came along in a backpack, and you were sure when a bird was hit that you'd done it with your little gun."

Leif doesn't comment, but Heidi giggles. Carla looks over at her.

"Heidi," says Carla, "you're holding your gun wrong. See Leif next to you? Your gun is pointing at his head. Put the gun over your other shoulder. That's right."

The hunters are hungry after a morning of hard work, and the dogs need a rest. After feeding the panting dogs and giving them water, they gobble down their lunches. Then they rest, picking burrs out of the dogs' fur and chatting about the hunt.

After resting up, the hunters head out again. Each of them can

Roger relaxes with the dogs during the lunch break.

legally shoot three pheasant a day. With four hunters, that means a dozen, and the morning hunt has resulted in only half that number. Heidi is tired and decides to stay by the cars and read.

By late afternoon, the hunters have bagged their limit. They gather together at the cars, give the dogs some more water, and drive back to the motel, tired but satisfied and happy after a good day.

Heidi takes time off from hunting to read.

—5

HUNTING
FOR DEER

*T*he Coxes live out in the country and have only to drive a short distance to hunt deer. They know the area very well, so they are aware of where deer are most likely to be. When it is time to hunt, they put on their orange vests. Deer can't see color, so they are not aware of the bright color that is so noticeable to us. Then the hunters put their rifles in the car, bringing along only as many bullets as they think they'll need that afternoon. Heidi leaves her wooden gun behind – she is tired, since they got up at six that morning to hunt geese. But she goes along on the deer hunt to be with the family and to enjoy being out in the woods.

After getting out of the car, the family gathers around as Roger explains the strategy for the day.

"We'll hunt across this slope and drop down to the road – it's only about a mile and a half. We'll spread out. Heidi, you come with me. Leif, you take the center while Carla takes the upper part of the slope. This way we can drive deer to one another. Remember to be quiet and move slowly. The deer are more likely to be alerted by seeing our movement than by hearing us."

Roger maps out the deer hunt.

The Coxes spread out, moving quietly through the open woods. After walking a bit, Roger tests the wind. He whispers to Heidi, "The wind is coming uphill. We'll have to move over that way. We don't want the deer to catch our scent."

The two of them work their way slowly along the fence line. Every few steps, Roger stops and listens carefully, then uses his binoculars. It is hard to walk quietly through the dry grass, and Heidi has to lift her feet high so as not to rustle too much.

Carla heads off for the hunt.

Roger uses the binoculars
to scan for deer.

A deer can melt into the trees
so that it's hard to see if
it doesn't move.

Roger stops suddenly and swings the binoculars up to his eyes. He points up the slope in front. At first Heidi sees nothing, then she spots the deer.

"It's a doe," Roger whispers. "I can't shoot it — my permit is only for a buck."

The doe is looking right at them. It spots movement as Roger leans toward Heidi, and off it goes, waving its white tail as it leaps through the woods. The hunters move on, continuing to pause every few steps to look and listen.

Bang! A shot rings out. Roger runs forward a few yards, looking up the slope toward where Leif and Carla are hunting, but he sees nothing. No wounded deer comes running through the woods. They slow down again but now walk up the slope so they will meet the other hunters.

Soon they reach Leif.

"That was Mom who shot," Leif explains. "She was quite a bit in front of me. I didn't see any deer running away after the shot."

Now the three walk together and soon come across Carla, who is carefully searching the ground.

"It was right about here when I shot," she says. "I don't miss often, but I guess I missed this time. There's no sign of blood or hair anywhere around."

Everyone helps look for signs that a deer has been hit. No one wants to leave a wounded deer to die alone in the woods.

"Here's some deep hoof marks in the ground — must be where it took off after I shot," says Carla.

"Look over here," calls Roger. "This is a buck scrape. The bucks paw at the ground and make these marks during the mating season. They leave their scent, probably so other bucks will know that another buck is in the area."

After making sure that Carla has missed, the family spreads out again and continues the hunt. Heidi stays with Roger.

"Look, Heidi," Roger whispers. "Over in that tree – there's a big woodpecker with a bright red head." The two of them watch

Roger, Heidi, and Leif discuss the shot they heard from Carla's gun.

A buck scrape.

as the woodpecker pounds its beak into the tree, then flies off through the woods.

The family meets again on the road. Roger and Heidi have spotted a couple of does, but Leif and Carla haven't seen a thing.

"Let's hunt through the draw over there," suggests Carla. "I've seen bucks in there several times."

It is getting late and Heidi is tired, but the family decides Carla has a good idea, so they head over to the draw.

"Leif, you stand here at the end of the draw. We'll drive the deer toward you. But if your mother or I have a chance at a good

Heidi looks through the binoculars at a woodpecker.

When Heidi has the binoculars, Roger uses the scope on his rifle to look for deer. Notice that his finger is not on the trigger.

shot, we'll take it, of course. You only have one direction you can shoot safely — straight ahead. If you shoot and miss, your bullet will lodge in the slope on the other side where it won't cause any trouble."

This time Heidi goes with Carla. Within five minutes a shot is heard.

"Come over here, I hit him!" yells Roger. They all run over to where the deer was standing when it was hit. Roger searches the ground for signs.

"Look — there's hair on the ground and blood on these pine needles," he points out. Roger carefully follows the tracks where he can see them, looking for more blood.

"Here — a drop of blood. The buck went this way." Even

Roger shoots; his finger is on the trigger.

Roger shows the children blood on some pine needles.

A telltale drop of blood shows which way the deer went.

though the animal was shot in the heart and is close to death, there is little blood.

In a few yards, they catch up with the buck, lying peacefully on the ground, dead.

Roger takes out his knife to dress the animal. "It's important to take out the internal organs quickly after killing game," he explains. "Otherwise, the meat can take on an off flavor." He works quickly, pointing out the different organs to Heidi.

Roger, Carla, and Leif take turns dragging the deer to the car.

Roger guts the deer. The deer's inside organs will be left for the ravens, magpies, and coyotes.

Carla and Leif drag the deer to the car.

They tie the buck on the roof and head home. Roger and Leif
hang the deer from the garage ceiling.

"We'll let the carcass hang here in the cool garage for a few
days to age before cutting it up and freezing the meat," explains
Roger. "Some people think it's more tender when it's hung
properly."

Everyone is tired but pleased after a successful day in the
woods. Roger helps Carla fix a dinner of pheasant bagged earlier
in the season and fresh vegetables from the garden. The family
sit down at the table and enjoy their meal together, chatting

Roger and Carla fix dinner after a busy day's hunting.

The family sit down to enjoy their meal.

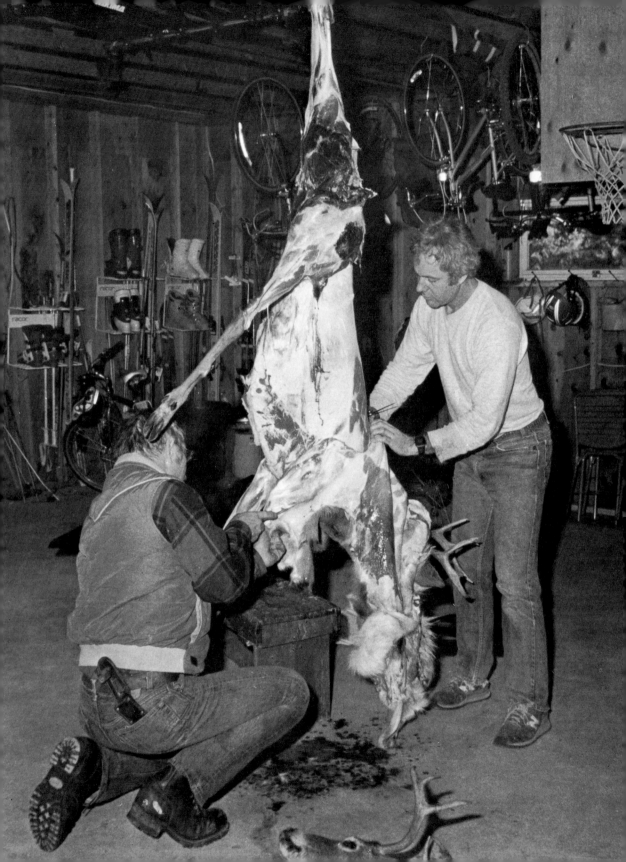

about the day's adventures and looking forward to the next hunt.

Several days later, Roger and his father skin the deer and cut the meat up, carefully removing extra fat. They wrap the roasts and steaks for freezing and grind the scraps for hamburger. Thanks to the deer, the Cox family will have fine meat for winter meals, and they are grateful.

Roger and his dad skin the carcass before cutting up the meat. The hide will be sold for a few dollars for making leather.

Commandments for Hunters

Hunters need to keep rules of safety and ethics in mind. As an aid to remembering these important considerations, lists of "commandments" have been created. The following two lists are from *Washington Hunter Education Student Handbook, Firearm Safety Training Program* (Seattle, WA: Outdoor Empire Publishing, Inc., 1976).

Ten Commandments of Firearm Safety

1. Treat every gun with the respect due a loaded gun.
2. Watch that muzzle! Be able to control the direction of the muzzle even if you should stumble.
3. Be sure the barrel and action are clear of obstructions and that you have only ammunition of the proper size for the gun you are carrying.
4. Be sure of your target before you pull the trigger; know identifying features of the game you hunt.
5. Unload guns when not in use. Take down or have actions open; guns should be carried in cases to the shooting area.
6. Never point a gun at anything you do not want to shoot; avoid all horseplay with a firearm.

7. Never climb a fence or tree or jump a ditch with a loaded gun; never pull a gun toward you by the muzzle.
8. Never shoot a bullet at a flat, hard surface or water; at target practice be sure your backstop is adequate.
9. Store guns and ammunition separately beyond the reach of children and careless adults.
10. Avoid alcoholic beverages before or during shooting.

Hunter's Ethics (Compiled by the National Rifle Association)

1. I will consider myself an invited guest of the landowner, seeking his permission and so conducting myself that I may be welcome in the future.
2. I will obey the rules of safe gun handling and will courteously but firmly insist that others who hunt with me do the same.
3. I will obey all game laws and regulations and will insist that my companions do likewise.
4. I will do my best to acquire those marksmanship and hunting skills that assure clean, sportsmanlike kills.
5. I will support conservation efforts that can assure good hunting for future generations of Americans.
6. I will pass along to younger hunters the attitudes and skills essential to a true outdoor sportsman.

Index